What Were You Thinking?

For Mom. You have always been there to teach me important lessons in life. Thank you for always being there for me.

A Story about Learning to Control Your Impulses

BOYS TOWN
Press

Boys Town, Nebraska

Written by **Bryan Smith**

Illustrated by **Lisa M. Griffin**

Published by the Boys Town Press
13603 Flanagan Blvd.
Boys Town, NE 68010

For a Boys Town Press catalog, call **1-800-282-6657**
or visit our website: **BoysTownPress.org**

Publisher's Cataloging-in-Publication Data

Names: Smith, Bryan (Bryan Kyle), 1978- author. | Griffin, Lisa M. (Lisa Middleton), 1972- illustrator.

Title: What were you thinking? : a story about learning to control your impulses / written by Bryan Smith ; illustrated by Lisa M. Griffin.

Description: Boys Town, NE : Boys Town Press, [2016] | Audience: grades 2-5. | Summary: Third grader Braden loves to be the center of attention. His comic genius, as he sees it, causes his friends to look at him in awe. But when his ill-timed jokes and actions result in interrupting class or hurting others, it's time for a lesson about impulse control.--Publisher.

Identifiers: ISBN: 978-1-934490-96-9

Subjects: LCSH: Impulse--Juvenile fiction. | Decision making in children--Juvenile fiction. | Egoism in children--Juvenile fiction. | Attention-seeking--Juvenile fiction. | Interpersonal relations in children--Juvenile fiction. | Children--Life skills guides--Juvenile fiction. | CYAC: Attention-seeking--Fiction. | Decision making--Fiction. | Egoism--Fiction. | Self-perception--Fiction. | Interpersonal relations--Fiction. | Conduct of life--Fiction.

Classification: LCC: PZ7.S643366 W53 2016 | DDC: E--dc23

Printed in the United States
10 9 8 7 6

Boys Town Press is the publishing division of Boys Town, a national organization serving children and families.

Hi, my name's Braden and I'm in the third grade.

Just so you know, I'm probably the funniest kid in my school.

SERIOUSLY!

I have made some kids cry and almost wet their pants because they were laughing so hard.

510

WELCOME

BACK

Anyway, this year school started the same way it does every year.

The teacher explains the rules.

We practice the rules.

And then we practice them some more.

Don't teachers realize third graders know how to follow the **rules?**
Well, on Friday, I realized why we practice the rules.

My teacher began class by saying,

"*Good morning, boys and girls.*

Today we *are going to...*"

That's when it just happened.... I shouted out,

"Talk about how AWESOME I am!"

The class giggled. My teacher, Mrs. Vickerman, said, "Whoa. Braden, we have rules to follow in class. Is interrupting me when I'm talking to the class following the rules?"

"No, I guess it isn't being respectful," I answered.

"Right! Remember, the first day of school we talked about what those rules look like in class, and we said *one way to show respect is to raise your hand if you have something to say,* and calmly wait for the teacher to call on you. That is one way that we control our impulses."

"Control our WHAT?

I'm sorry, Mrs. Vickerman, but that sounds like grown-up talk."

Mrs. Vickerman smiled and said, "They are big words, but what they mean is that sometimes our bodies are telling us to do things, and we have to decide whether or not to do them."

Later on, Mrs. Vickerman pulled me aside. She asked,
"When you shouted out, saying we were going to 'talk about how awesome you are,' what were you thinking?"

"Well, I thought it would be really funny."

*"Right, but did that make the situation **better** or **worse**?"*

I sat there for a second, then sighed and said, **"Worse."**

Mrs. Vickerman explained there are times to be funny and times to be serious at school. She asked me, "When is it a good time to be funny at school?" **"I don't know. Maybe lunch, recess, and free time."** "Right."

Mrs. Vickerman gave me
a card with four easy
steps to follow before saying
or doing something.

In our class

#1   Stop what you are doing.

     Think about what you
     are going to say or do.

#3   Decide if it will make the
     situation better or worse.

#4   Choose the behavior that
     makes the situation better.

In our Class

#1 Stop what you are doing.

#2 Think about what you are going to say or do.

#3 Decide if it will make the situation better or worse.

#4 Choose the behavior that makes the situation better.

This didn't seem too hard. I told Mrs. Vickerman I was sorry and would think before doing things from now on.

Later that day, in P.E., we were playing a new dodge ball game. **The only rules were you could not hit kids in the face, and you could not go on the other team's side.** My team was ahead and things were going great.

Out of the corner of my eye, I saw Amanda sneak over to our side and hit one of our players with a ball. Like a cheetah, I sprinted over to Amanda and threw a ball right at her face!

Just as the ball was about to hit her, Coach called out, "Braden, get over here right now!" I saw Amanda on the floor crying and knew this was not going to end well.

Then I heard the same words again,

"What Were You Thinking?"

I explained how I was mad Amanda cheated and that's why I hit her with the ball. Coach did not look happy, and told me I needed to control my impulses. Coach asked if hitting Amanda with the ball made the situation *better* or *worse?*

"Worse," I whispered.

He pulled out the tips card from Mrs. Vickerman and asked if I followed any of the steps. I realized I didn't even follow step **#1 Stop what you are doing.** Controlling my impulses might be harder than I thought!

That day when I got home, my parents already knew about what happened at school. Mom and Dad said we would be practicing controlling our impulses at home and they had a copy of the card Mrs. Vickerman gave me. "Oh great," I sighed.

In our Class

#1 Stop what you are doing.

#2 Think about what you are going to say or do.

#3 Decide if it will make the situation better or worse.

With all that happened at school,
I was surprised to see Mom was
making cupcakes for me.

Yum!

As they were cooling off on
the counter, I went in like
a hungry bear.

I ate 12 cupcakes and then had a huge tummy ache.

Mom came in, looking shocked, and asked, *"What in the world happened to your brother's birthday cupcakes for his class?"*

Uh oh. Maybe those weren't for me.

"Braden, you know you are supposed to ask permission! And with everything that happened at school today, **what were you thinking?"**

"I was thinking about how good they would taste."

"Did eating those cupcakes make the situation **better** *or* **worse?"**

"Well, they did taste good," I mumbled.

"I'm sure they did. But overall, did that make the situation for you, your brother, and me **better** *or* **worse?"**

"Worse," I said as I lowered my head.

We went over the card Mrs. Vickerman had given me **AGAIN.**
On top of that, I had to help Mom make more cupcakes instead of playing my favorite video game.

Not a fun night.

Why were these four steps so hard to follow?

A few days later at school it finally clicked! I was being my usual hilarious self with my friends at lunch. We were having a great time. Then I felt something mushy and wet smack me in the head. A kid from another class threw some Jell-O at me and his whole table was laughing!

I immediately thought, he just messed with the wrong person –
time to teach him a LESSON!

23

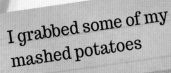

I grabbed some of my mashed potatoes

and got ready to throw a mashed potato fastball at his head. I reached my arm **Waaay back** to get full speed. As my arm was about to go forward, I stopped! I got this weird picture in my head of that card.

STEP #2

STEP #3

I asked myself, **Is this going to make the situation better or worse?** I knew the answer, and though it was hard, I decided to just raise my hand over my head to get the teacher's attention.

STEP #4

Mrs. Vickerman came over, and I explained what happened. She went and talked to the other boy and he had to go to the principal's office to finish his lunch.

Whoa, was I just able to control my impulse?

This made me feel good about myself.

Later in class, Mrs. Vickerman pulled me aside. She said, "I noticed you had mashed potatoes in your hands when you raised your hand today at lunch. Something tells me you weren't planning to eat those!"

I smiled and said, **"Yeah. I was going to hit that boy in the head with them, but decided it would be better to talk to you about it since it's one of the rules of the cafeteria."**

She laughed and said, *"So, what were you thinking?"*

Stay out of trouble.

"I was thinking I am sick of getting in trouble and for once wanted to make the right choice."

"That's great! And your good choice did make the situation better this time. You even followed all four steps!" **"Yep,"** I said. **Maybe I was becoming an impulse expert!**

CHECKERS

OCEAN QUES...

BLAST OFF!

oys

That night when I got home, my parents asked my brother and me to pick up our toys. And he just left his remote control car – the one he **NEVER** lets me play with – right in the middle of the floor!

28

Now, I am not going to lie to you. I thought for just a second this might be a good time to take my brother's remote control car and hide it in my closet. But then again, **would an impulse expert do that? I knew what the right thing to do was, so…**

29

... I walked into my brother's room and gave him his remote control car. My brother said,

"Thanks a lot, booger brain."

At first I got mad, and then I just laughed. I may be becoming an expert in controlling my impulses, but I'll never be able to **control** my brother!

Teaching Children to Control Impulses

When you're a child, it's not easy controlling your impulse reactions. Kids do things before they think all the time. Here are some easy tips to help you teach a child how to think before they act.

1. Many students with impulse control issues have a hard time dealing with their frustration or anger. Teach these children ways to calm down before responding to a situation (deep breaths, count to 10, stretching, etc.).

2. Children are always looking up to the role models in their lives. Make it a point to control your impulses and even share out loud your thinking during those situations.

3. Children need to understand it is not always appropriate to act on their thoughts. Help your child learn to filter possible consequences for what he is thinking of doing. **"Will behaving this way make the situation better or worse?"**

4. Support your child in recognizing her impulsive behaviors. Many times she may not even realize what she is doing.

5. Students with impulse control issues many times invade other people's personal space. Help your child understand other people's points-of-view and understand exactly what personal space is. Using a hula-hoop is a good visual to help children understand this concept.

6. Encourage lots of exercise to help active children control their impulses.

7. Help your child realize there are consequences to all of our actions (both positive and negative). Role-play situations to help prepare your child to respond appropriately.

8. Catch your child doing the right thing. Give him specific positive feedback when he controls his impulses.

For more parenting information, visit boystown.org/parenting.

BOYS TOWN®
Parenting

31

Boys Town Press books by Bryan Smith
Kid-friendly books for teaching social skills

Executive FUNction

My Day Is Ruined! — *A Story for Teaching Flexible Thinking* — Written by Bryan Smith, Illustrated by Lisa M. Griffin
978-1-944882-04-4

Downloadable Activities
Go to BoysTownPress.org to download.

Of COURSE It's a Big Deal! — *A Story about Learning to React Calmly and Appropriately* — Written by Bryan Smith, Illustrated by Lisa M. Griffin
978-1-944882-11-2

OTHER TITLE: What Were You Thinking?

It Was Just Right Here! — Written by Bryan Smith, Illustrated by Lisa M. Griffin
978-1-944882-20-4

TIME TO GET Started — *A Story about Learning to Take Initiative* — Illustrated by Lisa M. Griffin, Written by Bryan Smith
978-1-944882-31-0

When I couldn't get Over it, I learned to Start Acting Differently — *A story about managing SADness* — Written by Bryan Smith, Illustrated by Lisa M. Griffin
978-1-944882-22-8

Is There an APP for That? — Written by Bryan Smith, Illustrated by Katie Wigh — *Hailey Discovers HAPPiness through Self-Acceptance*
978-1-934490-74-7

WiTHOUT LiMiTS
dream • connect • soar

Downloadable Activities
Go to BoysTownPress.org to download.

EMPATHY is My Superpower! — *A story about showing you care* — Written by Bryan Smith, Illustrated by Lisa Griffin
978-1-944882-29-7

MINDSET MATTERS — Written by Bryan Smith, Illustrated by Lisa Griffin
978-1-944882-12-9

Kindness Counts — *a story for teaching random acts of kindness* — Written by Bryan Smith, Illustrated by Brian Martin
978-1-944882-01-3

IF WINNING ISN'T EVERYTHING, WHY DO I HATE TO LOSE? — Written by Bryan Smith, Illustrated by Brian Martin
978-1-934490-85-3

The National Parenting Center — Seal of Approval

BOYS TOWN® Press

For information on Boys Town and its Education Model, Common Sense Parenting®, and training programs:
boystowntraining.org | boystown.org/parenting
training@BoysTown.org | 1-800-545-5771

For parenting and educational books and other resources:
BoysTownPress.org
btpress@BoysTown.org | 1-800-282-6657